Copyright © 2001 by Michael Neugebauer Verlag, Verlagsgruppe Nord-Süd Verlag AG,
Gossau Zürich, Switzerland
First published in Switzerland under the title *Der Kern*
English translation copyright © 2001 by North-South Books Inc.

First published in the United States, Great Britain, Canada,
Australia, and New Zealand in 2001 by North-South Books,
an imprint of Nord-Süd Verlag AG, Gossau Zürich, Switzerland
Distributed in the United States by North-South Books Inc., New York

Library of Congress Cataloging-in-Publication Data is available.
The CIP catalogue record for this book is available from The British Library.

ISBN 0-7358-1407-4 (trade binding) 10 9 8 7 6 5 4 3 2 1
ISBN 0-7358-1408-2 (library binding) 10 9 8 7 6 5 4 3 2 1
Printed in Germany

For more information about our books, and the authors and artists
who create them, visit our web site: www.northsouth.com

A Michael Neugebauer Book
NORTH-SOUTH BOOKS
New York / London

THE SEED

Written and Illustrated by Isabel Pin

Translated by Rosemary Lanning

Once upon a time–in a small, distant part of the great, wide world–there were two tribes, the Scarabs and the Chafers. A border divided their two lands, and neither tribe ever crossed it.

Then, one day, something happened. An object suddenly fell out of the sky. To the Scarabs and the Chafers, it looked like a strange, rolling rock. They wondered where it had come from and what it could be.

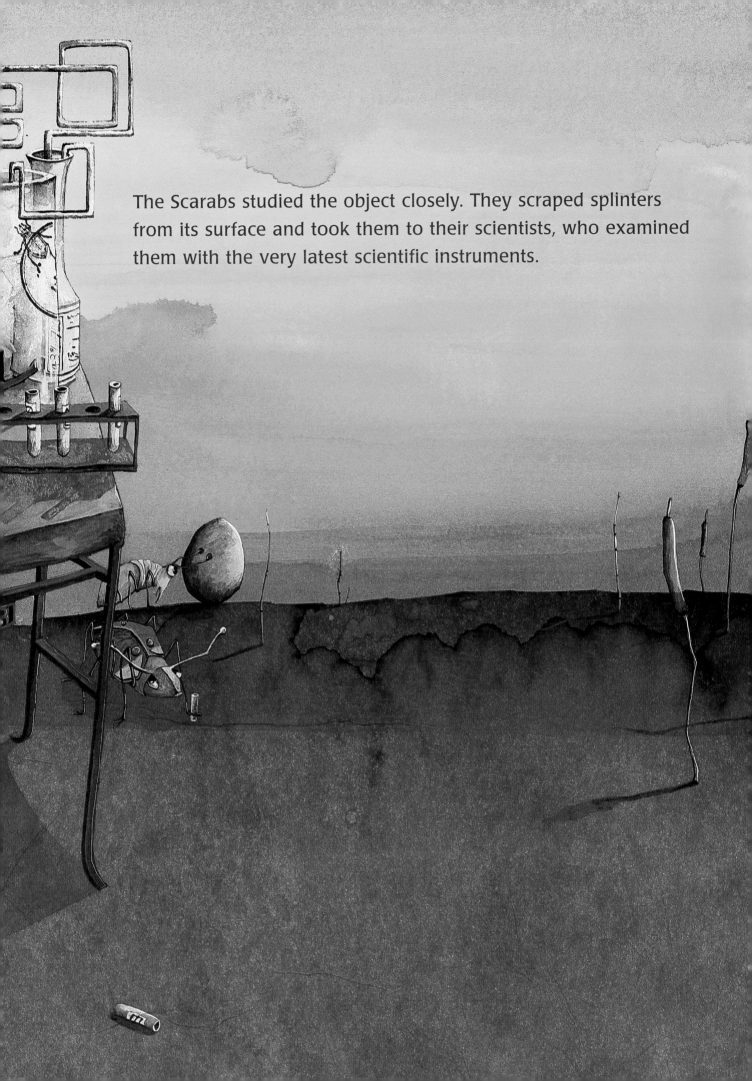

The Scarabs studied the object closely. They scraped splinters from its surface and took them to their scientists, who examined them with the very latest scientific instruments.

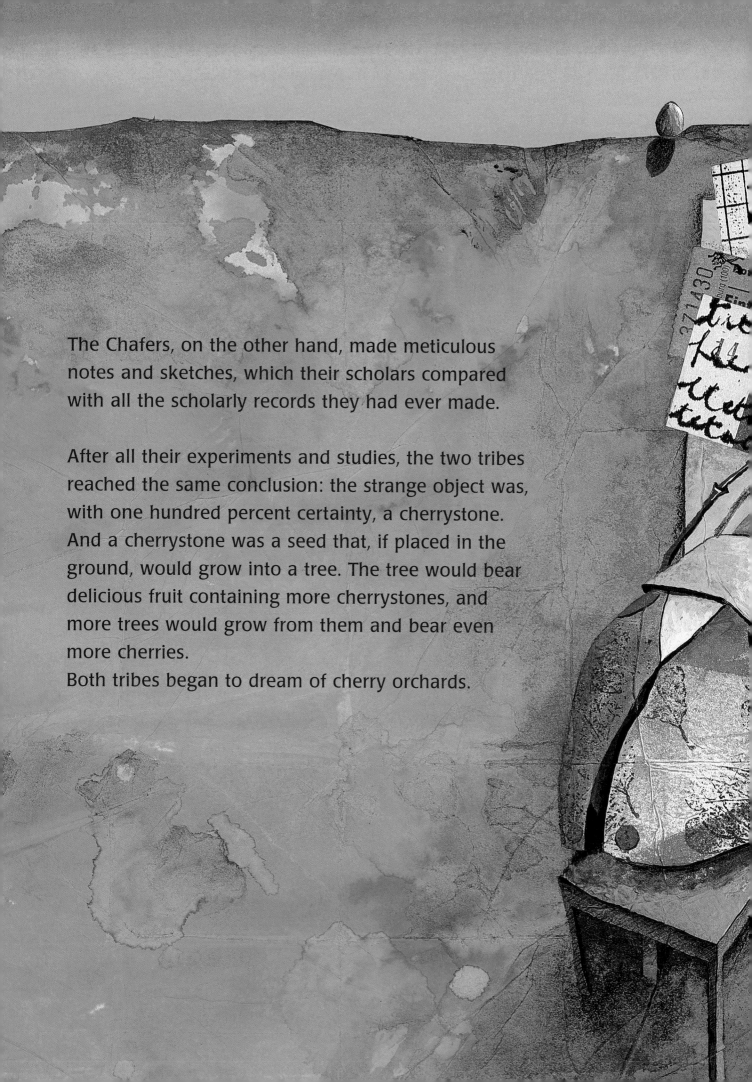

The Chafers, on the other hand, made meticulous notes and sketches, which their scholars compared with all the scholarly records they had ever made.

After all their experiments and studies, the two tribes reached the same conclusion: the strange object was, with one hundred percent certainty, a cherrystone. And a cherrystone was a seed that, if placed in the ground, would grow into a tree. The tree would bear delicious fruit containing more cherrystones, and more trees would grow from them and bear even more cherries.
Both tribes began to dream of cherry orchards.

There was only one problem. The cherrystone had come to rest right on the border. Neither tribe could claim complete ownership. And neither tribe was willing to renounce its share.

The Chafer and Scarab kings both ordered secret missions to drag the cherrystone over to their side of the border, but the cherrystone would not budge.

So the king of the Scarabs summoned his subjects and loudly accused the Chafers of trying to steal the cherrystone.
The Chafer king made the same accusation against the Scarabs. Neither admitted attempting to steal it himself.

"This means war!" announced the two leaders.
"We must fight to win this seed for ourselves!"
Neither the Scarabs nor the Chafers were enthusiastic
about the idea, but they reluctantly agreed.

"Our leader must be obeyed," they told
themselves. And from that moment, the two tribes
were enemies.

Both sides prepared for war with great inventiveness.
They kneaded clay and shaped it into bomb cases, constructed
catapults which could be aimed with great precision, designed
new cannons, spears, and nutshell shields.

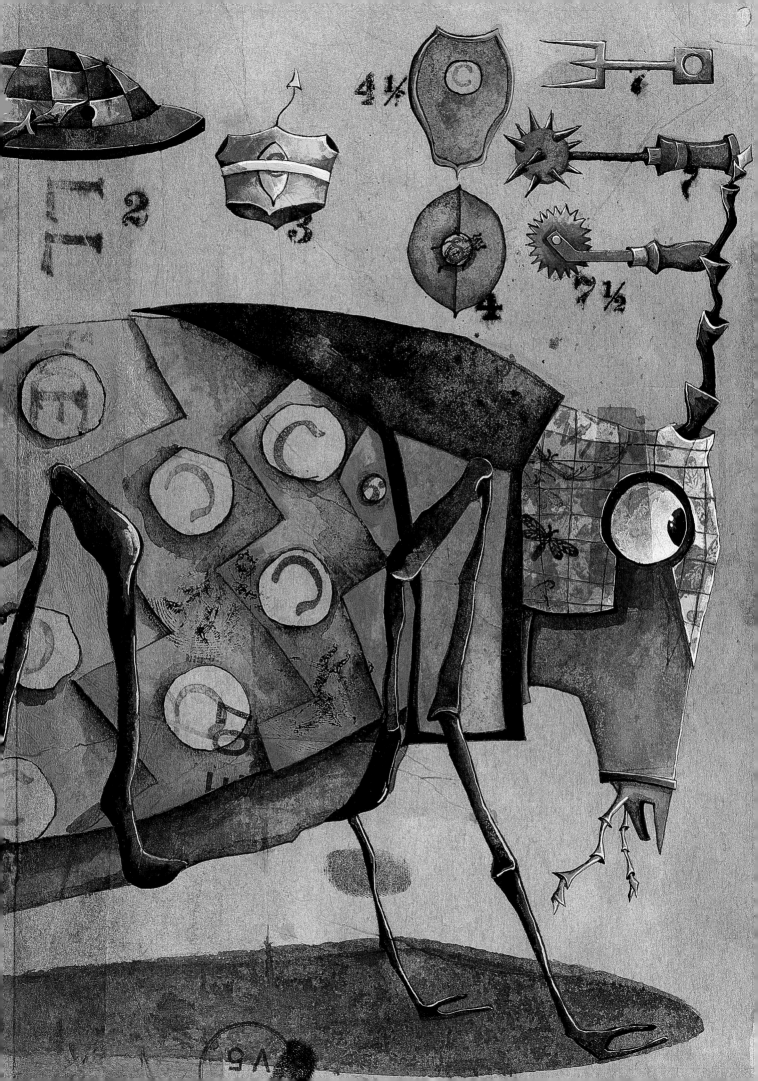

Military experts drew up crazily complicated plans of attack. They measured and mapped the smallest features of their territory, taking note of every pebble and tuft of grass in case they might affect the outcome of the battle.

Years passed. No one stood guard over the cherrystone.
They were too busy arming themselves for the battle to claim it.

Tirelessly they dug trenches, sank shafts, and built a network of tunnels to secretly invade enemy territory.

At last the two tribes were ready for war. The Chafers on one side and the Scarabs on the other marched up to the border. Then, just as their leaders gave the order to attack, they suddenly noticed . . .

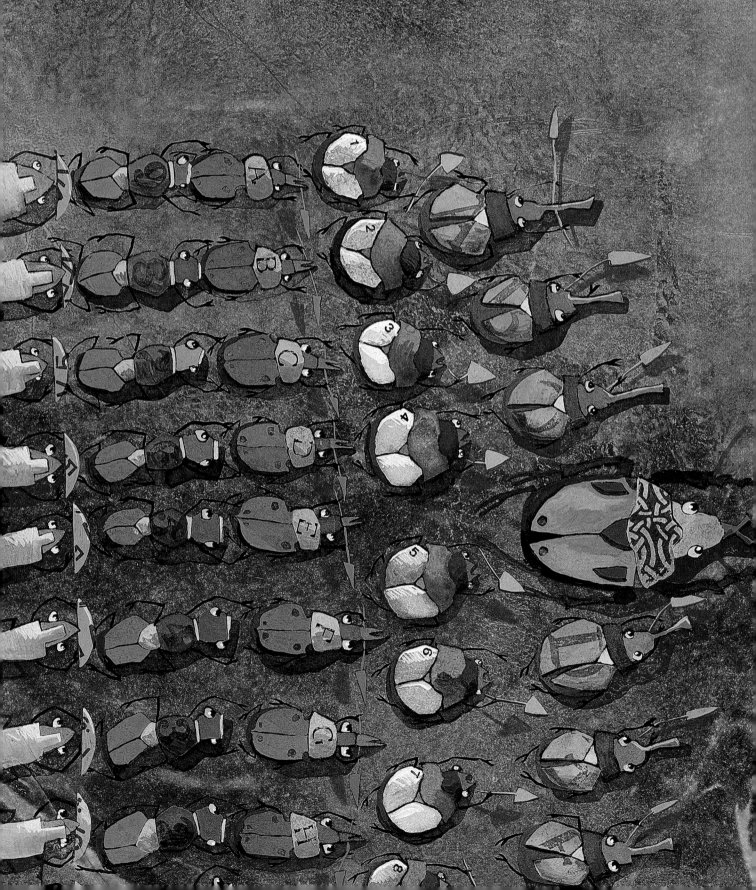

that the cherrystone was gone. It had buried itself in the ground, taken root and grown into a small cherry tree, covered in blossoms. The Scarabs and the Chafers looked at the tree, thought hard, and saw that there was no reason to fight now. The tree was growing right on the border, its branches reaching out over both lands. They could share its beauty and the fruit it would bear.

And so the great war between the Scarabs and the Chafers was cancelled, and the two tribes lived in peace and harmony ever after.